JIMMY SNIFFLES
THE SUPER-POWERED SNEEZE

Librarian Reviewer
Allyson A. W. Lyga, MS
Library Media/Graphic Novel Consultant
Fulbright Memorial Fund Scholar, author

Reading Consultant
Elizabeth Stedem
Educator/Consultant, Colorado Springs, CO
MA in Elementary Education, University of Denver, CO

STONE ARCH BOOKS
MINNEAPOLIS   SAN DIEGO

Graphic Sparks are published by Stone Arch Books,
151 Good Counsel Drive, P.O. Box 669,
Mankato, Minnesota 56002.
www.stonearchbooks.com

Library of Congress Cataloging-in-Publication Data
Nickel, Scott.
  The Super-Powered Sneeze / by Scott Nickel; illustrated by Steve Harpster.
  p. cm. — (Graphic Sparks. Jimmy Sniffles)
  ISBN-13: 978-1-59889-316-8 (library binding)
  ISBN-10: 1-59889-316-5 (library binding)
  ISBN-13: 978-1-59889-411-0 (paperback)
  ISBN-10: 1-59889-411-0 (paperback)
  1. Graphic novels. I. Harpster, Steve. II. Title.
PN6727.N544S86 2007
741.5'973—dc22   2006028026

Summary: Jimmy Sniffles' super powers lie in his nose. So what happens when his
spectacular sniffs are wiped out by cold medicine? Nothing, and that's the problem. It
sure would be disastrous if a super villain – say, Dr. Von Snotenstein – took advantage of
Jimmy's weakness and escaped from the dream dimension. It would be even worse if the
doctor had powerful Snot-Bot machine-terrors to help him conquer the world. Now that's
nothing to sneeze at!

Art Director: Heather Kindseth
Graphic Designer: Brann Garvey

1 2 3 4 5 6 11 10 09 08 07 06

Printed in the United States of America

JiMMY SNiFFLES
THE SUPER-POWERED
SNEEZE

by Scott Nickel   illustrated by Steve Harpster

CAST OF CHARACTERS

Dr. Von Snotenstein

Jimmy Sniffles

Guinea Pigs

Snot-bot

Petey the Poodle

Oops!

Something's wrong with my nose.

I sneeze when there's danger, but this cold has made my sneezes super powerful!

18

21

23

Back to the dream dimension I go! But we'll meet again, Jimmy Sniffles!

Back at Jimmy's house . . .

I defeated Dr. Von Snotenstein and made it back home without getting caught by Mom.

ABOUT THE AUTHOR

Born in 1962 in Denver, Colorado, Scott Nickel works by day at Paws, Inc., Jim Davis's famous Garfield studio, and he freelances by night. Burning the midnight oil, Scott has created hundreds of humorous greeting cards and written several children's books, short fiction for *Boys' Life* magazine, comic strips, and lots of really funny knock-knock jokes. He was raised in Southern California, but in 1995 Scott moved to Indiana, where he currently lives with his wife, two sons, six cats, and several sea monkeys.

ABOUT THE ILLUSTRATOR

Steve Harpster has loved drawing funny cartoons, mean monsters, and goofy gadgets since he was able to pick up a pencil. In first grade, instead of writing a report about a dog-sled story set in Alaska, Steve made a comic book about it. He was worried the teacher might not like it, but she hung it up for all the kids in the class to see. "It taught me to take a chance and try something different," says Steve. Steve landed a job drawing funny pictures for books. He used to be an animator for Disney. Now, Steve lives in Columbus, Ohio, with his wonderful wife, Karen, and their sheepdog, Doodle.

GLOSSARY

allergic (ah-LUR-jik)—if you are allergic to things, you might sneeze, cough, or get a rash. People can be allergic to plants, dust, furry animals, or evil supervillains.

archenemy (arch-EN-uh-mee)—someone's very worst enemy

dimension (duh-MEN-shun)—an environment or surrounding where things live and move

radar (RAY-dar)—a cool, high-tech way to find objects by using invisible radio waves. Radar cannot be used, however, to find missing homework.

rodents (KOH-duntz)—small furry creatures with sharp front teeth for cutting and chewing. Rodents make good pets, unless you are a tree.

schnozz (shnahz)—a funny word for the nose. Other good words for nose are **beak**, **bazoo**, **honker**, **snoot**, and **whiffer**.

ultimate (UL-tuh-mit)—the most, or best, or biggest of something. An ultimate rodent would have a giant schnozz, and if it was allergic to humans, it would have a monster sneeze. ACHOO!

SNIFFLES ON SNEEZES

Teachers hate sneezes! Why? Because, according to some experts, students with colds and sniffles miss about 189 million school days each year!

The most famous sneeze on record took place on January 7, 1894. That's when inventor Thomas Edison made one of the world's first movies — about a man sneezing!

We humans sneeze to get rid of bad stuff in our bodies. The brain can sense a lump of mucus in our nose when we have a cold or an allergy. The body knows it shouldn't be there, so it tries to expel, or reject, the mucus with a powerful, eye-watering sneeze.

There is no cure for the common cold.

Gingerbread was an invention of the ancient Greeks. Long ago, the Chinese borrowed the recipe and used it as a medicine for colds. It didn't work, but it sure tasted good!

Be glad that you didn't have a cold in ancient Rome. The Romans use to treat their sneezes by soaking an onion in hot water and then drinking the mixture. Eeeew!

How fast is a sneeze? The average sneeze travels at about 100 miles per hour. According to some scientists, people sometimes blurt out a super-sneeze at 630 miles per hour. Yikes! Get out of the way!

DISCUSSION QUESTIONS

1. What is your favorite way to spend the day when you're home sick from school? Is there anything special that you do? Would you rather be home sick, or at school? Why?

2. Can you think of anything else Jimmy could have done to make himself sneeze?

3. Why does Dr. Von Snotenstein want to give everyone a cold that only his medicine can cure?